BuUuUrP!

DO NOT TAKE YOUR DRAGON TO DINNER

WRITTEN BY JULIE GASSMAN
ILLUSTRATED BY ANDY ELKERTON

Capstone Young Readers
a capstone imprint

It's a special occasion! It's time for a **treat**.
Time to dress up and go out to eat.

But carefully consider your dinner's guestlist.
For, my dear friend, I must simply insist . . .

A rude guest like a dragon disturbs everyone.
He barges right in. He spoils the fun.

A wing in your face! A tail in a drink!
And worst of all, that distinct dragon **STINK!**

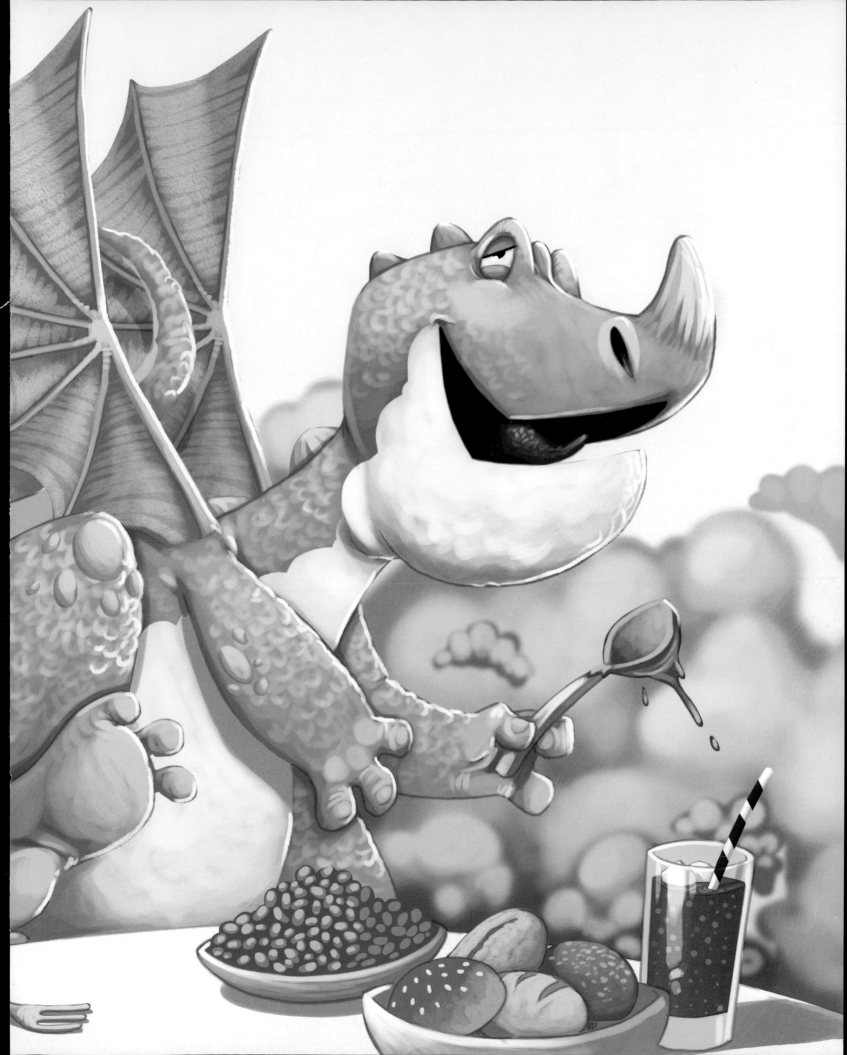

Waiting for food, she'll get really bored.
And then her behavior cannot be ignored.

She'll grab for your phone. She'll crawl on the floor.
She'll stand on the table and let out a **ROAR!**

You may believe that once food is in sight,
your dragon will sit and be so polite.

But he'll pick up his bowl.
He'll drink with a **slurp**!
And then he'll let out a fiery **burp**!

SO DO NOT TAKE YOUR DRAGON TO DINNER!

Dragons are known for taking big bites.
When the food spills back out
it's a **terrible** sight.

She pounds on the table.

She plays with her food.

She picks at her fangs.
She's very, very rude!

But my dragon is so very special to me.
Celebrate without him? It simply can't be!

He's part of my family. Part of my **heart**.
What can I do so we don't have to part?

Ah, my friend, I sense your frustration.
But dinner at home can be a grand celebration.

You can ask your dragon to help with the meal.
His flame can **sear**. His claws can **peel**.

He can set the table, put each dish in its place.
He can light the candles with incredible grace.

Then at dinner, practice being polite.
Sit still, use silverware, try not to ignite.

Ask him to use napkins, instead of his wings.
Remind him to ignore the phone if it rings.

Encourage him to close his mouth when he chews.
And be sure he remembers his pleases and thank yous.

Practice this often, and your etiquette beginner . . .

About the Author

The youngest in a family of nine children, Julie Gassman grew up in Howard, South Dakota. After college, she traded in small-town life for the world of magazine publishing in New York City. She now lives in southern Minnesota with her husband and their three children. Julie's favorite way to celebrate anything is with a delicious meal, with or without her dragon.

About the Illustrator

After fourteen years as a graphic designer, Andy decided to go back to his illustrative roots as a children's book illustrator. Since 2002 he has produced work for picture books, educational books, advertising, and toy design. Andy has worked for clients all over the world. He currently lives in a small tourist town on the west coast of Scotland with his wife and three children.

Do NOT Take Your Dragon to Dinner is published by
Capstone Young Readers, a Captone imprint
1710 Roe Crest Drive, North Mankato, Minnesota 56003
www.mycapstone.com

Copyright © 2017 Capstone Young Readers

Library of Congress Cataloging-in-Publication Data is available on the Library of Congress website.
ISBN: 978-1-62370-916-7 (paper-over-board)
ISBN: 978-1-4795-9888-5 (library binding)
ISBN: 978-1-4795-9176-3 (eBook pdf)

Summary: We know you shouldn't take your dragon to the library, but what about taking him out to dinner? After all, dragons need to eat too! But with fiery breath, flapping wings, and pointy spikes, that might not be a good idea!

Designer: Ashlee Suker

Printed and bound in China.
010418F17